GO

DIEGO

GO!

ANIMAL RESCUER

Science

Photo page 9 © Tim Davis/Corbis

Published by Scholastic Inc., 90 Old Sherman Turnpike, Danbury, CT 06816

ISBN 0-439-90704-7

Printed in the U.S.A.

First Scholastic Printing, January 2007

SOUTH POLE RESCUE!

by
Christine Ricci

illustrated by
Alex Maher

SCHOLASTIC INC.

New York   Toronto   London   Auckland   Sydney
Mexico City   New Delhi   Hong Kong   Buenos Aires

Diego was working at the Animal Rescue Center when he heard about an animal that needed help. "A mother emperor penguin hurt her foot," said Diego. "We need to help her make the long journey across the ice to find Daddy Penguin, who has been keeping their egg warm!"

Diego opened up his Field Journal.

"Emperor penguins are birds," Diego read. "They cannot fly, but they are great swimmers. Both parents take turns caring for the chick."

Diego closed his Field Journal. "I've got to find out more," he declared as he hurried off to find his sister, Alicia.

Alicia checked her computer. "After the mommy penguin lays her egg," she read, "the daddy penguin keeps it safe and warm on top of his feet. While the daddy penguin is caring for the egg, the mommy penguin makes a long journey to the ocean to find food."

"So we need to help Mommy Penguin get back to Daddy Penguin and their egg!" said Diego.

"Let's ask our special camera, Click, to help us find Mommy Penguin," said Alicia.

With Click's help, Diego learned that Mommy Penguin was in Antarctica, one of the coldest places on Earth.

"I'll go get the airplane ready!" said Alicia. *"¡Vámonos a la Antártida!"*

They soon found Mommy Penguin.

"I hurt my foot on some sharp ice," she explained.

Diego wrapped her foot in a special waterproof bandage.

As Diego and Mommy
Penguin trudged through the
deep snow, Diego had an idea.
"I bet Rescue Pack can transform
into something that will help us travel
in this snow! *¡Actívate!*"

Rescue Pack transformed into a
snowboard and Diego hopped on. Diego's
snowboard made a nice wide path through the
snow so that Mommy Penguin could flop down
and slide on her belly.

"*Wheeeee!*" said Mommy Penguin. "We emperor penguins love to slide on our tummies!"

"Uh-oh! Deep water!" said Diego, as they reached the bottom of the hill. *"Actívate!"* Rescue Pack transformed into a boat.

"Hop in, Mommy Penguin!" said Diego.
Mommy Penguin hopped into the boat. "We penguins
are super swimmers," she said.
"But I think I'll ride until my
foot feels better."

As Diego and Mommy Penguin reached the other side of the icy channel, a cold wind sprang up. "Brrr!" said Diego, pulling his warm coat closed. "Are you warm enough, Mommy Penguin?"

"Oh yes!" said Mommy Penguin. "I have feathers and a nice warm layer of blubber to protect me!"

Soon they heard loud cooing and singing. They were close to the nesting place!

"We made it!" said
Diego, as they reached the
top of a hill and looked down.
There below them were thousands
of emperor penguins. "But how will we find
Daddy Penguin in this big crowd?"

"I can recognize his special call," said Mommy Penguin. She listened carefully and then said, "He's over that way!"

Diego and Mommy Penguin made their way through the crowd of penguins. "There he is!" she shouted.

"¡Hola, Daddy Penguin!" called Mommy Penguin.
"¡Hola!" Daddy Penguin called back. "Look! Our egg
started to hatch. The baby will be here soon!"

Daddy Penguin looked hungry, tired, and very happy to see Mommy Penguin.

Just then, the baby penguin finished pecking
its way out of the egg.

"¡*Hola*, Baby Penguin!" said Diego.

"Peep! Peep!" said Baby Penguin.

His body was covered with fine, fluffy feathers. Now it was Mommy Penguin's turn to keep him safe and warm, while Daddy Penguin went to the ocean to find food.

"*¡Adiós* and *gracias*, Diego!" the penguins called.

"¡Adiós!" Diego called back. **"¡Misión cumplida!** Rescue complete!"

Nick Jr. Play–to–Learn™ Fundamentals
Skills every child needs, in stories every child will love!

colors + shapes — Recognizing and identifying basic shapes and colors In the context of a story.

emotions — Learning to identify and understand a wide range of emotions: happy, sad, excited, frustrated, etc.

imagination — Fostering creative thinking skills through role-play and make-believe.

123 math — Recognizing early math in the world around us: patterns, shapes, numbers, sequences.

music + movement — Celebrating the sounds and rhythms of music and dance.

physical — Building coordination and confidence through physical activity and play.

problem solving — Using critical thinking skills (observing, listening, following directions) to make predictions and solve problems.

reading + language — Developing a lifelong love of reading through high interest stories and characters.

science — Fostering curiosity and an interest in the natural world around us.

social skills + cultural diversity — Developing respect for others as unique, interesting people.

Science

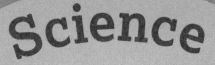

Conversation Spark

Questions and activities for play-to-learn parenting.

Diego and Alicia work together to help animals. Mommy and Daddy Penguin work together to hatch the egg. Have you ever worked together with someone? Draw a picture of it.

For more parent and kid-friendly activities, go to www.nickjr.com.

ENGLISH/SPANISH GLOSSARY
and PRONUNCIATION GUIDE

ENGLISH	SPANISH	PRONUNCIATION
Let's Go!	¡Vámonos!	VAH-moh-nohs
Antarctica	Antártida	ahn-TAR-tee-dah
Activate	Actívate	ahk-TEE-vah-tay
Hello	Hola	OH-lah
Good-bye	Adiós	ah-dee-OHS
Thank you	Gracias	GRAH-see-ahs
Rescue	Misión	mee-see-OHN
Complete	Cumplida	coom-PLEE-dah